Sudden Death of Thelma's Fiancé

Is it his pet snake or a murder case?

ROBERTELLO MATOUSEK

DEDICATION

This book is dedicated to my dear sister, Agnes.

CONTENTS

Acknowledgments I

1 Thelma—The Girl from Missouri 1

2 The Mother of Mischief 5

3 Thelma Falls in Love 8

4 A Shoe Disappears Mysteriously 15

5 Death of Thelma's Fiancé —Shrouded in Mystery 20

6 About the Author 41

ACKNOWLEDGMENTS

The persons most directly responsible for this book becoming a reality include three precious women in my life: Specioza my love, and my two daughters, Misha and Ella. Thank you for always being there for me.

1 THELMA—THE GIRL FROM MISSOURI

Thelma was born on 3 April 1993, near a small town called Ozark, 19 miles south of Springfield, Missouri. Her mother, Barbara O Purvis, was of Asian origin and worked as a model. She later left modeling clothes and become very religious.

Thelma's parents first met in a nightclub and later started cohabiting together. Her father was of Hispanic origin by the name of Thomas B Glass. Barbra and Thomas got misunderstandings after Thelma was born and separated when she was only two years old.

Barbara got a job in a clothing store in Wentzville about a 45-minute drive from downtown St. Louis. It was not easy to juggle full-time employment and the responsibilities that come with being a mother. She sometimes slept at 11.00 pm and had to wake up at 5.00 am.

Barbara became one of Jehovah's Witnesses and got married to Robert S Janousek, a native Hawaiian. They got married when Thelma was aged 5, and she lived with them until her teens.

Barbara produced two other children with Robert, a boy, and a girl, named Scott and Mary respectively. Barbara took the time to teach her three children bible principles, but Thelma never accepted the worship of God.

When Thelma was 13 years old, something happened at school that troubled her. She decided to discuss it with her mother. "A boy touched me inappropriately," Thelma told her mother.

Barbara laughed softly and asked: "What do you mean?"

"He touched my breast," said Thelma.

"Did you tell the teacher?" asked the mother.

"No, I didn't. It is the third time the boy did it. I think he likes me."

"Sure he does," her mother replied.

"He said my breasts are like tennis balls, ready to play ball. And that my eyes are like the sun."

"What else did he tell you?"

"He said that when I turn and look at him, my gaze is like a flash of lightning, which leaves him helpless. I like what he says about me. But what does he mean when he says I am ready to play ball?"

"Thelma, you are in transition from childhood to womanhood. You have started developing a woman's calves, and boys will start admiring your body."

"What do you mean?"

"As I explained, you will soon see the moon."

"Yes, I remember what you said. I will soon get my first period. I am scared," Thelma said, looking worried.

"There is nothing to worry. As I explained, it is part of growing up. Your body is going to change to enable you to be a mother. In contrast, a male body develops to be able to father children."

"What changes do boys experience?"

"You see Scott's private parts?" her mother said, pointing to Thelma's half-brother. Scott was on all fours playing will his toy car, unconcerned.

"Yes, it is small and weak," Thelma said laughing. "His body grows like a rocket, but his organ's growth rate is slower than a snail."

"When he reaches puberty, it will start becoming big so that he can father children," said her mother, her face expressionless.

"When a man sees or gets in contact with a woman, his organ receives an abnormal blood supply," Thelma's mother continued, struggling to stay calm. "A flaccid organ can be slightly longer than your middle finger. When erect it becomes bigger and about ¾ your middle finger longer."

"Why does it become longer and bigger than is normal," Thelma asked innocently.

This part was the hardest for Barbara to explain to Thelma. Nevertheless, she knew that if she did not tell her, someone else would do so. She didn't want her daughter to read it on the internet, media or try to find out because of curiosity.

"When a man places his organ into the female's private parts it is very pleasurable for both of them," said Barbara. "But Jehovah God only allows sexual relations between married people. The Bible condemns immorality."

"Why is it not allowed between those who are not married?"

"When you engage in sexual relations when you are not married, you can become pregnant and drop out of school. Your young lover is usually not able to shoulder the responsibility. The boy more often than not disappears, leaving you to carry the burden. Above all, it is a sin against God. Ignoring God's law has caused lots of problems to teens."

"Were you married to each other when you gave birth to me? Why did you separate?"

"No, we were not married. I met your father at a nightclub, and he took away my innocence," said Barbara. "But your coming was a great blessing. You are such a lovely daughter." A tear rolled down her face.

"I did not mean to hurt your feelings. I am sorry."

"It's alright," said her mother. "You will find girls at school who tell you to use contraceptives."

"What are contraceptives?"

"A contraceptive prevents pregnancy. Some contraceptives come in the form of pills which, when swallowed, prevents a woman from conceiving. But the issue is not to prevent pregnancy; it is to preserve moral purity."

Barbara wiped away the tear from her cheek and looked directly at her daughter. She saw how young and innocent she was and felt pity for her. She was growing into her teens and had to face temptations single-handedly.

"Thelma," Barbara said and placed her hands on her daughter's shoulders. "Thelma, you should let no man mislead you. Never accept to sleep with a man before you get married to him. Once you sleep with him, he will not see the need to marry you."

Thelma nodded. She could sense the seriousness in her mother's voice. Thelma knew that her mother wanted her to lead a happy, successful life. Her mother wanted the best for her.

"I was naïve and accepted your father's advances. Life has never been the same since. I have got many problems after that. I dropped out of school; the embarrassment was overpowering. Stay away from boys who are not ready to marry you. Put off sexual relations and marriage until you have finished school."

At age 17, Thelma left her mother and foster-father and started living with her uncle, Edward C Purvis, in Denton, a city about 25 miles from Dallas, Texas. Edward had lost his wife and daughter in a car accident and wanted someone to help him around the house and farm.

Edward forced Thelma to work for many hours before and after school. A soybean and dairy farmer, Edward owned a 25-acre farm stocked with 60 dairy cattle, a tractor, and other farm equipment.

Thelma woke up at 5.00 am every day and helped to milk the cows. Every evening, when she came back from a nearby day school, she assisted with various tasks on the farm including watering and feeding animals and cultivating the fields.

She learned how to plow and harvest soybeans using a tractor and how to use other agricultural equipment to carry out a full range activity on the farm. She gained skill in dealing with workers and in record keeping and maintenance. The training she acquired proved helpful later in life.

Thelma did not have enough time for her homework and other school activities, and her school grades suffered. As a D-student and because of the meager resources available to her she could not join the best universities. Her mother encouraged her to pursue a course in office administration.

2 THE MOTHER OF MISCHIEF

John S MacDonald was born in the United Kingdom. His parents migrated to the United States when he was five years old and settled in Texas, USA.

MacDonald served in the army and fought in the Vietnam War. In 1990, he joined the Federal Bureau of Investigation (FBI) to combat violent crime, in particular, to track and arrest fugitives who crossed state lines.

Following the first 1993 World Trade Center bombing in New York City, MacDonald joined the anti-terrorism unit. MacDonald traveled extensively around the world, following September 11, 2001, attacks on the World Trade Center. He assisted in the ensuing flurry of investigations and the formulating of counter-terrorism measures.

MacDonald resigned from the FBI in 2009 and started a consultancy firm offering services to investigative journalists. He settled in Texas and decided to give more time to his wife and get involved more in the upbringing of their two sons, Jonathan MacDonald Sr. and Johan MacDonald Jr.

Jonathan and Johan were entirely different. Johan was a risk taker, aggressive and very curious. He was canning and liked experimenting with new things. He was always an A-student and very creative. On the other hand, Jonathan was a B-student, but empathetic, patient and compassionate.

A case in point is when Jonathan's cat called Katz was run over by a car. Jonathan was devastated. He refused to eat for two days and wept until the neighbors came. Nothing could comfort him for many days.

Another event that illustrates that Jonathan and Johan were poles apart in their outlook and behavior involved the family car. When Johan was ten years old, Macdonald's family friends organized to take all their kids to the Austin Zoo, located on the southwest edge of Austin.

But Johan hated going to the zoo. He played sick and refused to go. Jonathan remained at home to look after his brother, while their parents went with the group.

The MacDonald's left the family car at home. Johan stole the car key from his parent's bedroom and attempted to drive. As he made through the gate, it scratched the side of the car, severely damaging the door.

He left the car at the gate and called Jonathan. "What have you done, Johan?" asked Jonathan. "You have wrecked the car."

"Do not tell Dad," Johan pleaded. "Let us move the car back into the parking lot. We shall tell dad that I knocked it with my bicycle."

As they were arguing about the best way to handle the situation, Mr. Jack Thompsons, a neighbor two blocks down the road was passing. "What is the problem?" he inquired. "Who told you to drive the car? You are too young to drive."

"Dad told the mechanic to take the car for repair, but he crashed it into the gate," Johan lied. "He has gone to get some spare parts and left us here to guard the car. We have been standing here for about 30 minutes, waiting for him to return. Can you help us to move the car back to the parking lot?"

Mr. Thompsons knew Jonathan and Johan as well-mannered children. He believed their story and drove the car back into the parking lot. "I doubt the mechanic will come back at all. Where are mom and dad?"

"They went to town," said Johan. "They will be here any time."

After Mr. Thompsons left, Johan removed all traces of paint from the gate. But he could not cover the crime. When MacDonald examined the car, he knew that someone had crashed it into some barrier.

MacDonald's anger grew hot. "Jonathan I see the car was damaged. Who allowed you to drive it?"

"Johan crashed the car against the gate," said Jonathan.

"It is Jonathan who told me to drive out and buy ice cream," said

Johan.

Jonathan failed to prove that he had nothing to do with the accident. Both received a punishment, but the Jonathan's was more onerous than Johan's because of his age.

MacDonald noticed that his sons were interested in information technology and encouraged them to study it at the university. Johan majored in software development, and coding and Jonathan excelled in database management.

MacDonald saw the potential in his sons and decided to form MacTec10, a software development company dealing with the development of computer applications for companies and high-end individuals. He invested his time, effort and all savings in the company to get it running.

MacTec10 started picking up after Jonathan and Johan completed their university education. Located in Austin, Texas, MacTec10 took off like a rocket. Johan's Android App that linked businesses to clients was a significant boost to the company.

The App was based on the 80/20 rule and helped companies to identify minnows from whales, sharks, and dolphins. It allowed companies and individuals to concentrate on the big customers (whales, sharks, and dolphins) and not waste time on small ones (minnows).

Soon MacTec10 was the talk of town and businessmen were rushing to make orders for custom and generic Apps. The labor force moved from 10 to 50 within two years. The company's annual revenue increased to $1.3 million within the same period, and the company made a decent profit of $450,000 by the end of the third year.

3 THELMA FALLS IN LOVE

Thelma first met Johan in Austin, while attending a conference on Apps to track and monitor the movement of livestock. They sat at the same table at lunch, and while conversing about general things the conversation drifted to operating agricultural machinery.

Johan was always interested in making Apps for agricultural equipment, but never got the time to study them carefully. After about 10 minutes Johan and Thelma realized that they had many things in common. Both of them enjoyed horse racing, American football, and swimming.

Johan was impressed by Thelma's beauty and intelligence. She could comprehend difficult concepts quite quickly and analyze complex situations. They exchanged business cards and agreed to stay in touch.

Johan was plump, stocky, and shorter than average with a pot belly. He had a round face and long nose, goat-like beard and mustache. His eyes were large and set deep in their sockets. His hair was thick and dark. His appearance reminded Thelma of her teacher at the college.

Johan called after a week and advised Thelma to apply for the position of Administrative Assistant in MacTech10. The job offered better working conditions compared to her uncle's farm. A month later she joined MacTec10 and moved to Austin.

Thelma disliked the way Johan treated subordinates, although he never managed her harshly. He shouted at them and refused to honor their requests, even when they were in line with company policy. He was arrogant and impatient.

One day Johan took Thelma out for an evening and told her that he was interested in her. Thelma was not impressed, but she never showed it because Johan was her boss. Life in the city was better than on the farm.

Johan wasted no time and told everyone that they were pushing out with Thelma. He started showering her with gifts. Thelma was confused. She did not know how to say to him that she had no romantic love for him. At the same time, she hated pretense.

One day Thelma wanted to buy a phone. Johan took Thelma to PetalMobile; a custom made phone company based in Austin. Thelma chose a 5.5" Motorola and the seller offered to engrave it with Thelma's initials on the back cover within an hour.

Johan picked up the phone but delivered it to Thelma the next day, in the afternoon. He claimed that he forgot the phone at his residence. Thelma noticed that the flashlight switched on automatically at awkward times, but she passed it off as a bug.

Jonathan was quite the opposite. He was tall and slender, yet muscular. His medium size eyes were deep brown and beautiful. Gentleness, politeness, honesty, and intensity emanated from them. Jonathan and Johan were miles apart in appearance and behavior, as though they from different parents.

One day Jonathan and Thelma met in the canteen. Thelma was leaving the cafeteria when Jonathan walked in. He held the door for her and smiled. "You look depressed these days," he said. "Is there any way I can help?"

"It is nothing."

He handed her a piece of paper. "Here is my private phone number. I will call you on Sunday."

There was something about Jonathan that she could not understand, something mysterious. Everything he said seemed right and compelling. Thelma smiled and just said: "Alright."

The next day, Johan took out Thelma to a lovely Park in Austin. He held Thelma's hands, looked straight into her eyes and said: "I love you, Thelma."

Thelma felt no emotion whatsoever. "Thank you, but I am not ready for love. My time has not yet come."

"What do you mean?"

"I will remain your friend, but I am not ready for a close relationship."

Johan let go of her hands and looked away in frustration. After a few minutes, he asked: "Is it because of Jonathan?"

Thelma only shook her head. How does he know that Thelma had a soft spot for Jonathan? "Why do you say that?"

"I am just suspecting, my brother always fares better with girls than me," said Johan. He removed his spectacles and started cleaning them with a hankie. "Maybe I am jealous. I am in love with you. It is a pity you have no feelings for me."

"There is nothing between Jonathan and me."

Jonathan called Thelma two days after her encounter with Johan, and they talked for hours. It was as if they had known each other for decades. Thelma told Jonathan about her family and how he came to be in Austin.

Thelma knew that she had started the slippery path towards Jonathan's arms—she knew she had fallen in love. It was a frightening thought. How would Johan react when he found out? Could Thelma lose her job? Did she have a fallback position?

"Be careful not to get involved in a close relationship with someone with no intention of getting married," warned Thelma's mother, Barbara. "It will be like putting your hand in bowel from which you cannot pull your hand. Love is stronger than life."

Thelma could not resist Jonathan. She was ready and itching for his arms. She naively thought that she could pull back if things did not work out.

After two months Thelma and Jonathan had reached a point of no return. Although they tried hard to conceal their feelings for each other, keen employees at the office could see that there was something between the two of them.

The closer Thelma and Jonathan became, the harder Johan tried to persuade Thelma. The waves of tension between Johan and Jonathan began to manifest, although in subtle ways.

One day Macdonald caught Jonathan gazing at Thelma as she walked into her office. Macdonald called his son Jonathan to his office and warned him about Thelma. "Thelma is Johan's girl," he said. "Keep your hands off her to avert disaster. Remember that our company is young and vulnerable."

Jonathan sat there, calm and composed. "There is nothing serious going on," he lied. "I think it is just a crush. It will soon resolve itself. I will add no more firewood."

"Very well," said MacDonald. "Please keep your distance, for love is blind to the power of reason. Sometimes you are all hat and no cattle, the reason why I had to talk to you. Pull back before it is too late."

Jonathan could not bear a day without talking to Thelma. He knew that falling in love did not always mean peace and pleasantness. Sometimes it hurts and evokes recklessness. His father was right. Love is like a train. When it starts rolling, you cannot stop it without causing damage.

You can't see love.

It cannot be touched.

You can't smell love.

You only feel it in the heart and act to prove it.

Jonathan knew that he had fallen in love. He could feel it in his heart. Thelma had become part of him. The day he held her in his arms and followed the calves of her body with his hands, he crossed a line of no return. He accepted Thelma's love and was ready to pay the price, however high.

Jonathan was on Thelma's mind all the time. At one time she whispered into her phone that nothing would separate her from Jonathan.

Love is strange. It judges nothing until there is a misunderstanding. It assumes that your partner is perfect. But even when you detect something wrong, you tend to ignore it, until after you get married, or calamity strikes.

Jonathan and Thelma fell in love the day they first saw each other. Their hearts were bound together before they talked to each other. Their passion strengthened day by day, into the heavens above. Maybe it will reach the stars, perhaps not.

"Jonathan," said his father, "will you not work today?"

Jonathan gathered his love rattled bones and left his father's office, lost in thoughts.

Jonathan sent a message to Thelma requesting her to meet him in the evening. They met at the Hampton Inn & Suites to discuss the days' events.

Jonathan booked a table in the gardens, in the private section.

"I love you, Thelma," Jonathan said. He pulled her close and held her tightly.

She trembled slightly when his body touched his. She felt her left breast move in her bra and was momentarily thrown off guard, as her body responded to his touch.

Thelma felt his organ against her thigh and remembered the words of her mother: "Never sleep with a man before marriage." She pulled away from him.

"What is it? Don't you love me?"

"I love you, Jonathan," she whispered, her eyes half-closed. "I have never loved a man this much."

"Then why are you running away from me?"

"It is wrong to sleep with you before we get married. Obtain me legally, and after that, you can do anything you want with me."

Jonathan remembered that Thelma was raised as a Witness, although she did not progress to baptism. "I still love you. I will wait until we get married."

Someone was watching Thelma and Jonathan from the balcony above. He was mad that Thelma was "cheating" on him. "Jonathan has gone too far to be left unpunished," he said softly. "He will have to pay for holding Thelma in his arms."

Jonathan and Thelma left in different vehicles. A black Mercedes followed Jonathan's car, keeping a reasonable distance in order not to be detected. After visiting a friend in Austin, he passed by Northcross Mall to buy the next week's supplies. Unaware that he was under surveillance, Jonathan didn't notice the black Mercedes that parked three cars away in the third row.

Jonathan came back from the supermarket and opened his car to put stuff into the boot. All of a sudden two beautiful women came out of the car parked nearby and started exchanging sharp words.

Before long they started fighting. Jonathan felt compassion for the weaker woman and went over to help her. When they saw Jonathan, they stopped fighting, sat in their car and quickly drove away. Jonathan looked at the car as it sped away and shook his head, confused.

He opened his car and sat in the driver's seat. Before he knew what was happening, he felt a rope around his neck. At first, he thought that a thief had entered his car. The attacker was pulling hard on the line, literally choking him.

"Stay quiet and listen carefully," said the attacker, in a dead, flat and croaky voice. "I have been sent by Thelma's ex-boyfriend. If you want to die, go ahead with your silly relationship with Thelma. You touch her again, you are as good as dead. Do you understand?"

He felt a sharp pain run through his shoulder and warm liquid flowing down his arm. The attacker pulled harder on the rope. Jonathan felt as if a piece of meat was stark in his throat, and felt pain in his chest. After a few seconds, he lost consciousness.

He gained consciousness when his phone rang. There was blood on his shirt and trousers. He tried to answer the phone, but the pain in his shoulder was unbearable. He realized that the attacker had inflicted a wound on his shoulder. He was grateful that the attacker did not cut off his hand.

It was the same scary voice. "Howdy man? Leave Thelma alone. You will die a slow, painful death if you touch her again."

The caller used a telephone booth. Jonathan locked the doors of his car and drove home, his hands trembling. He had many questions on his mind. Thelma had never mentioned an ex-boyfriend or any other person with whom he had a close relationship.

It dawned on him that he was up against a well-organized gang. He suspected that the two women did not start fighting by coincidence; they wanted to divert his attention.

He tried to get Thelma out of his mind but to no avail. His heart and his very being were bound up with Thelma. The two of them were like Siamese twins; he could not free himself from Thelma, without getting hurt. What could he do?

Jonathan told Thelma about the attempt on his life, but to his father and Johan, he said nothing. He lied to them that he had fallen in the bathroom and hurt his shoulder.

The attack on Jonathan complicated things for the two lovebirds. At the bottom of her heart, Thelma suspected that it was Johan trailing them, but there was no evidence. They decided to be more careful and use a coded language to communicate.

They started meeting in a secret garden behind the Catholic church as the mass was in progress. Thelma disguised herself, traveled by bus and passed through the rear gate to reach the gardens. As for Jonathan, he left the church auditorium as if he was going to the washrooms and slipped through into the garden.

John Baptist, a local Catholic priest and Jonathan's former colleague at school, helped to arrange the meeting point. The place worked perfectly for some months. It was a perfect meeting place, and they used it to organize meetings elsewhere.

Their love, genuine and sincere, grew stronger and matured. They put off marriage for a year to observe Johan's reaction and plan accordingly. So strong was their love that they were prepared to leave the United States and live somewhere else.

4 A SHOE DISAPPEARS MYSTERIOUSLY

It was Monday morning.

Thelma called Jonathan, but he was not picking up his phone. Thelma smiled as he imagined Jonathan's arms around her and his lips against hers.

Thelma had last met Jonathan on Saturday afternoon at Crystal River Inn, a hotel located in San Marcos City, about 30 miles South of Austin.

Thelma and Jonathan used separate vehicles to go, and each booked their room to avoid suspicion. After checking in, Jonathan sneaked into her room, and they had fun. She intentionally left the door open, to guard against going 'overboard.'

Thelma left San Marcos for Austin at around 6.00pm. Jonathan started half an hour later. He had an appointment to meet Johan for dinner in Austin. The agenda included the discussion of an App they were working on along with how to open new marketing channels in the Far East.

Thelma and Jonathan agreed never to call each other over the weekend or after work. Their relationship was sweet like stolen wine. Just the mere act of holding hands would excite them beyond words. But it was difficult to suspect that their relationship went beyond work.

"Perhaps he is in the washroom," she reasoned. She knew she had fallen in love. But what if Johan found out? It would be a disaster. Johan loved Thelma. But Thelma's heart was hooked to Jonathan.

She called after 30 minutes; there was again no answer. She was concerned. Jonathan was always with his phone. "Something is wrong," muttered Thelma.

She got into her car and drove to Jonathan's residence. She pressed the secret code, and the gate swung open. She noticed that the outside lights were still on. She looked at her watch. It was 8.35 am.

She rang the doorbell, but there was no response. She tried the door, and it was unlocked. She was suspicious. When she entered, she called Jonathan's name, no answer.

Her heart skipped a beat. Something was wrong. She ran upstairs and found her lover lying on the couch in his study, motionless.

"Jonathan! Jonathan!" No answer. Jonathan's eyes were lifeless and stared at the ceiling, but he was still breathing. She started for the door but stumbled over something and fell. She looked at Jonathan again and pulled out her phone to call for help, but she dropped the idea.

She heard the familiar hissing from the cage. It was Jonathan's pet snake. The cage door was open, but she could not see the snake. It dawned on her that the snake was on the loose.

It must have bitten Jonathan, she thought.

She made an alarm and fled the room.

She could not call an ambulance.

She could not call the police.

She ran out of the house, got into her car, closed the gate and drove off.

She called Johan. "There is a client who wants to see Jonathan urgently. I have called his number several times, it was ringing, but no one answered. Can you please try to find out?"

Thelma could not control herself. She was shaking uncontrollably. She parked the car, but could not get out of the driver's seat. Jonathan was her life. How could she live without him?

She called Johan again after five minutes. "Have you called Jonathan," she asked her voice trembling.

"No, what's wrong? Jonathan sometimes comes late at work," said Johan unconcerned.

"But he answers my phone calls," she said and hung up. She could no longer control herself. She broke down and cried.

She had to act fast to save Jonathan from the snakebite. She could not call the police or an ambulance because she did not want Johan to know that she was at Jonathans' early in the morning.

Thelma was in a dilemma. Every passing minute brought Jonathan's death closer. "He decided to call the Jonathan's Dad, the MD of MacTec10.

After composing herself, she tried to convince the MD to go to Jonathan's house. "Tell the customer that I will be in office in 20 minutes," replied MacDonald.

Her heart sunk. "No, but I think there something wrong with Jonathan. He always answers my phone calls. I have called three times within 20 minutes; he doesn't answer," she said.

Thelma's voice gave her away. Macdonald remembered the time he caught Thelma holding hands with Jonathan in the washroom corridor and warned Jonathan to leave Thelma alone. It was dangerous for his two sons to be in love with the same woman.

Thelma was a beautiful girl. From the sole of her foot to the top of her head, she had no visible defect. Her blue eyes and upturned nose made her look like a princess. Her body calves were those of a model from the movies.

Johan recruited her as his secretary at MacTec10. She was a naive girl from the countryside. After two years at MacTec10, she had transformed into a beautiful, smart, intelligent, and persuasive woman.

One day, McDonald was embarrassed when Johan caught him staring at Thelma. Both men looked at each other, the father and his son, and Macdonald behaved as if nothing had happened. "She has a beautiful voice...," Macdonald thought.

Thelma's voice jolted Macdonald out of his dream world. "Will you go to Jonathan's urgently?" Her voice urgent, tearful, almost begging.

"Let me go there immediately," said McDonald.

When he reached the gate, it was locked. He rang the bell. No answer. He decided to call Johan.

"Please give me the secret code for Jonathan's gate. There seems to be a problem," MacDonald told his son Johan.

"Sure," Johan said. "I will send it to your folder using the blockchain."

McDonald was very observant. He had worked in the FBI before he started MacTec10. The front door was open. As he entered the sitting room, he noticed a woman's shoe in the sitting room. Its position was as if it fell off a woman fleeing in a hurry.

Macdonald found Jonathan lying on the couch in his study, unconscious. He breathed with difficulty, and his face was pale. Macdonald called for an ambulance.

"Your brother is unconscious," he told Johan on the phone.

"Let me arrange to come as soon as possible," replied Johan.

As MacDonald paced the room while waiting for the ambulance, he heard the familiar hissing of a puff adder from its cage. He noticed that the pen was open. It was Jonathan's pet snake.

He tiptoed and closed the cage door and sat down, looking at the wall ahead of him. But he did not see the wall. He was worried about MacTec10. He called a snake Vet for help.

"I will be there in about half an hour," said the Vet.

The ambulance arrived after 13 minutes. After examining Jonathan, the Doctor declared him dead. On further examination, the Doctor discovered two puncture wounds oozing watery blood on Jonathan's left leg, about six inches to the side, below the knee.

The vomiting before his death and the swelling of his regional lymph nodes confirmed that he died from puff adder snake venom.

Macdonald broke down in tears. He loved his son. Although Johan was better at coding and design of new applications, Jonathan was an excellent manager and organizer.

Macdonald had warned him about keeping snakes. But Jonathan loved serpents, especially dangerous snakes. At one time he had a cobra and a black mamba. They were too dangerous, and he gave them up in exchange for the puff adder.

Jonathan's room overlooked a beautiful park behind the house. From Jonathan's study, it was difficult to see what was going on in the parking yard.

Johan arrived at the scene 5 minutes before the medical team.

He saw the woman's shoe, picked it up, wrapped it in a tablecloth, put it in his briefcase, and locked the suitcase in his car boot.

Johan left the gate open and sat in his car to make a telephone call. A few minutes later the medical team arrived.

None on the medical team paid attention to the two cars parked outside. Johan watched from inside his Toyota Land Cruiser and decided to go in after the team had left.

When Macdonald saw his son Johan, he started weeping uncontrollably. Johan gave him his shoulder, and they cried together.

"It seems the puff adder, his pet snake, bit him," sobbed MacDonald. "But why was the front door not locked? Why did Jonathan not call for help? What about the woman shoe? Those questions beg for answers."

"You found a woman's shoe, and the front door was unlocked?" asked Johan innocently. "Let me call the police."

Kitz, Jonathan's black cat, came into the room. She was a lovely cat, playful and alert. She jumped into Johan's hands, unaware that her master was dead.

When the police came, MacDonald briefed them about what he had seen when he first came in. However, they could not find the shoe. "Perhaps Kitz hid it somewhere," suggested Johan.

"Who came in after you?" asked the policeman.

"The doctor and two nurses came in and examined the body and left," replied MacDonald. They searched the whole house, but they couldn't find it.

"My name is Raphael," said the police officer. "Call me if you find anything."

The Police took the body to the Coroner for further investigations.

There was another cage with four compartments for keeping birds, small mammals, toads, lizards, and frogs. "Jonathan used to feed the snake on live animals," observed Johan tearfully. "He loved serpents, but look they have killed him."

His father said nothing.

5 JONATHAN'S DEATH—SHROUDED IN MYSTERY

Johan hated Thelma. He knew all the dirty secrets between her and the diseased. But this was not the time to open the can of warms. He pretended that he knew nothing.

On the other hand, Thelma was depressed, angry and disappointed. Why did Jonathan have to buy the snake? Did she contribute to her death by not calling for the ambulance straight away?

She loved Jonathan so much. But their relationship was hindered and going nowhere because of Johan. She did not like Johan, although she pretended to do so.

After the burial, Thelma told Johan that she was going home to her mother for a week. Johan did not care; he felt cheated, betrayed. How could she be such a double-dealer? He wished that she had died instead of Jonathan.

The coroner's report concluded that puff adder snake venom had killed Jonathan. But there were two anomalies: 1) the puff adder's fangs had gone thicker than expected and 2) they found traces of isoflurane, a drug commonly used as a general anesthetic, in Jonathan's blood.

"Jonathan kept isoflurane for sedating his reptiles before taking them to the Vet doctor for treatment," Johan told the police. The police recovered a small bottle of isoflurane from Jonathan's house and took it away as an exhibit.

The police report concluded that there was no evidence of foul play in Jonathan's death. The case was closed, but the police agreed to reopen it if they unearthed proof to the contrary.

Nevertheless, Macdonald was not convinced. The woman's shoe that disappeared mysteriously and the open door kept haunting him. He decided to hire a private investigator to look further into the case.

MacDonald hired Paul Mackenzie, a no-nonsense former FBI agent, and investigative journalist.

Paul Mackenzie started work immediately. He searched Jonathan's house for clues. The house was in a quiet neighborhood at 2264 Sundown Lane, Austin TX 78749. It was a beautiful two-story property, enclosed in a fence with a medium compound.

The snake cage was six-foot square, large enough to accommodate a python. It had a pegboard on top for ventilation, cardboards on the sides and a glass in front.

The door opened on the side and was lockable. There was enough room to clean and move around it. Coconut fiber covered the floor of the cage. The cage had two compartments for smooth feeding of the reptile.

There was a bright light above the cage, which automatically switched on and off during the day and night respectively to mimic the light changes in the wild. The pen was well ventilated, with a dark hiding place and pool like depression with water.

There was nothing to suggest that the reptile could escape by mistake. Paul Mackenzie noted the name of the cage manufacturer on the nameplate and looked up the telephone number from the directory.

He inquired if the manufacturer knew any puff adder snake supplier in Texas. The cage manufacturer indicated there is no official supplier. He noted that dangerous snakes were imported, mainly from South Africa, using special permits.

Two days later he located and interviewed the coroner who carried out the autopsy. He had a small office on the 3rd floor of an office block in Georgetown, 25 miles to the north of Austin.

He always admired Georgetown city center; it is one of the most beautiful in the US. Georgetown is the home of several large industries including aerospace, bioscience, and life sciences.

"What do you mean when you say that the snake fangs went

deeper into the fresh than usual?" asked Paul Mackenzie.

"We scrutinized the wound," explained the coroner, "and found that the depth of the fangs and the angle of penetration were slightly different for each fang. It was as if the snake's fangs were lame. Each fang went straight ahead as if it was a needle."

"What was the spacing between the fangs?" asked Paul.

After checking the papers, he said: "14.5mm apart."

"Why didn't you put this information in the report?" Paul inquired.

"We are not experts on snakes," replied the coroner, "we just included what we thought was relevant."

Paul Mackenzie left the coroner's office in haste. He had to move quickly before the murderer destroyed evidence.

Paul Mackenzie drove south to Round Rock city, situated five miles to the south of Georgetown and 20 miles north of Austin. His Suzuki Escudo managed the journey in less than ten minutes.

As he drove past Dell Computers, he remembered a recent article that the 'City of Round Rock was the third on Nerdwallet's Most Affordable Places in America list.'

"Perhaps that is why Christopher McNeal," Paul thought, "the snake Vet who offered to look after Jonathan's serpent chose to live here."

"Good afternoon, Mr. McNeal," said Paul with a smile. "How is the veterinary business in Round Rock?"

"Great, and how are you," replied Christopher. "How can I help you this afternoon?" he asked. He had a worried look on his face. MacDonald had called and told him that a private investigator would visit him in connection with Jonathan's death.

"Mr. McNeal, what is the average length of a puff adder?" asked Paul.

"You can call me Christopher," he replied calmly. "The average length is one meter, but some heavyweights in the African wild can reach two meters."

"How toxic is the puff adder's venom?" asked Paul.

"Highly toxic," replied Christopher. "Puff adders kill more people in Africa than any other snake. It has two hollow curved fangs, which fold up against the roof of the mouth in a protective fleshly covering."

"How long does a person take to die when bitten?"

"Normally, it is 2-4 days, depending on the number of bites and volume venom injected," said Christopher. "The fatality rate from severe venom injections is about 52%."

"How long are the fangs?" asked Paul.

"It depends on the snake, its age and size," said Christopher. "The range is 5-20 mm."

"And the distance between the fangs?" asked Paul.

"It depends on the size," said Christopher. "The distance is less than 8mm for small snakes, 8-12mm for a medium sized snake and over 12 mm for a large snake."

"How do you rate Jonathan's puff adder?" Paul asked.

"It is medium," said Paul. "Come and see."

He led Paul to a large room. There were six cages, each containing a snake. "This is called the eastern coral snake," Christopher began, "and the other one over there is pigmy rattlesnake."

Jonathan's snake was in the last cage in the second row. Christopher went and picked up a small rat from another pen using a pair of tongs and threw it into the cage. The puff adder came out of hiding and moved towards the rat. It was about 0.85 m long.

Paul thanked Christopher for the information and left.

Paul tried to piece together the facts. The coroner told him that the distance between the puncture wounds was 14.5mm. That would be a huge snake, but Jonathan's is medium.

Furthermore, the snake fangs are 5-20mm long, and both follow the same angle of penetration into the fresh. The coroner said that the depth of puncture hole was 21mm and 23mm respectively, and each followed slightly different directions.

Puff adder venom kills a person in 2-4 days, depending on the dose. That means Jonathan must have been unconscious the whole of Sunday and no one bothered to call on him.

Something did not add up.

On Thursday, Paul Mackenzie went to interview Johan at the MacTec10 offices. He arrived at the offices at precisely 10.00 am.

"My name is Paul Mackenzie," he told the receptionist. "I want to talk to Mr. Johan MacDonald."

"Please go into the waiting room," said Thelma, "he will be with you in a few minutes."

After a few minutes, Johan came and took Paul Mackenzie to his office.

"I was commissioned by Mr. John MacDonald to investigate the mysterious shoe found at the residence of the deceased," Paul said, watching for Johan's reaction.

Johan was expressionless. His lips were tight. After some moments he said "What do you want from me? Is the death of my brother, not enough?"

"When did you last meet your brother before he died?"

"On Saturday evening," Johan replied, looking at the floor in deep thought. "We had dinner together."

Johan started crying. He got out a yellow handkerchief and wiped the tears from his eyes.

"Where did you have the dinner?"

"Austin Motel."

"When did you leave for home?"

"At 10.00 pm," said Johan looking at his watch. He seemed to be uneasy. "Is that all? I have a customer waiting."

"Did you use the same car or each drove home separately?"

"I took Jonathan home," he said while avoiding looking in Paul's eyes. "Jonathan had one bottle too many."

"Where did you leave him?"

"I helped him into his bedroom and closed the door behind him. I knew the lock combination of the front door to the house and main gate to his property. I locked the doors and left."

"Did you see him again before he died?"

"No."

"Thank you very much for your cooperation. I will contact you when I need more information."

They exchanged business cards, and Paul left.

Johan attributed Jonathan's death to alcohol abuse. Jonathan tried to feed the snake when he was drunk, and it bit him.

Paul called Mr. McNeal, the snake Vet. "Do snakes attack people without provocation?" he asked.

"No," said Mr. McNeal. "They only bite in self-defense, for example when you step on it. Otherwise, they stay away from humans."

Jonathan was found unconscious on a couch in his study. Did he lie on the couch after the snake bit him or did it bite him while on the couch? If the snake had bitten him in self-defense, it would have been on the forearm or hands. Instead, the puncture wounds were on his leg.

MacDonald, Johan's father and MD of MacTec10, was the first on the scene. He found the snake hiding in its cage, with the door open. Did it bite him and retreated into the cage?

That is an unlikely scenario. The cage had a 3-inch clearance underneath, which would be a perfect hiding place for it.

What about the woman's shoe? Whose shoe is it? Where did it go? The police searched Jonathan's house carefully, but the lost shoe could not be found.

Mackenzie asked his FBI friend Patrick Robertson to check out the security camera footage and find out who entered Jonathan's property between Friday and Monday. Patrick reported that hackers had tampered with the security system and erased the data for the period.

"Can we find the hackers," Paul asked.

"It is tough, but not impossible," said Patrick. "You need a significant amount of cash to hire someone to investigate."

Immediately, Paul suspected Johan. He studied coding at the university and designs MacTec10's best selling applications.

The security camera records would not help, it was a dead end.

Mackenzie was piecing together the pieces of the jigsaw, but many parts were still missing.

On Friday morning, he went back to visit Mr. Christopher McNeal.

"Please do me a favor," said Paul. "Call Mr. MacDonald and pretend that Jonathan's snake sick. Ask him for the address of the snake supplier. You can tell him that you want to get the catalog of medicines that can be used to treat the snake."

"Sure," said Christopher. "Why do you want the information?"

"I want to learn more about these snakes as part of my investigation. I would appreciate if you would put the phone in the conference mode."

Christopher was apprehensive, but picked the phone and called. "Thelma must have the address," said MacDonald. "Let me ask her to give it to you."

A few minutes after, Thelma sent the Vet this message:

Dorothy B Gordon,

Serp Ent, Inc

2028 Heuvel St,

Sterkspruit, 9762

Eastern Cape.

Tel: 083 897 1442

Paul Mackenzie flew to South Africa on Sunday. He did not inform anyone about the trip except his wife. He told his wife that he had urgent business to do and would be back Thursday morning.

Somehow Johan knew about the message Thelma sent to the Vet. He warned Thelma not to give out any more information about Jonathan without his consent.

Thelma was shocked. "I have not sent out any information."

"You sent the Vet information about the supplier of Jonathan's snake in SA."

"How do you know?"

"The Vet told me. Call him and tell him it is the wrong information."

Thelma felt insecure. Johan was reading her messages and possibly listening to her phone conversations.

"Why? Jonathan's snake must have a problem."

Johan lost his temper. "Why do you interview me? I expect you to obey orders. I am your boss."

Thelma could not believe it. She was confused. "It is the MD who told me to send the address."

Johan stormed out of Thelma's office.

On Friday afternoon, Paul Mackenzie visited MacTec10 offices to meet Thelma. He wanted to leave no stone unturned.

"I am Paul Mackenzie," he said as he sat down with Thelma in the meeting room. "When did you first meet Jonathan?"

"It was when I joined MacTech10."

"Did he have enemies?"

"No," said Thelma looking at her hands.

She started weeping.

"There is something you are not telling me. Did you love

26

Jonathan?"

"Yes," she sobbed. "Jonathan was my friend."

"Did he have enemies?"

"I don't trust you."

"Please trust me," he pleaded. "I want to find out the truth. There are still some unanswered questions about Jonathan's death."

"One day he was attacked as he entered his car after shopping at Northcross Mall," she said. "He told neither Mr. Macdonald nor his brother Johan about the attack."

"What was the motive of the attack? Was the attacker a thief?"

"I don't know," she lied.

"Was he injured?"

"The attacker tried to strangle him and inflicted a deep wound on his shoulder."

"And he didn't tell Johan?"

"Not even his father," she said.

Jonathan's death had exciting twists and turns that left Paul Mackenzie guessing. He would interview Thelma again when he came back from South Africa.

Paul Mackenzie touched down at Moshoeshoe International Airport, in South Africa at 10.00 am local time on Monday morning. He took a domestic flight to Quthing Airport, located 14 km from Sterkspruit, Eastern Cape.

He leased a self-drive car at Quthing Airport and drove straight to 2028 Heuvel St. He found Mrs. Gordon, the Managing Director of Serp Ent, in her office.

She was a pretty woman with big bums and breasts, and a winning smile. Paul liked her confident walk and handshake, and after a few minutes of meeting each other, they were chatting like they had known each other since childhood.

"My name is Paul Macadam, a businessman visiting from the US. I live in Austin, Texas. I once visited a friend of mine in Ohio, who owned a pet Gaboon Adder, measuring 1.5 meters. From that day I have longed to have my own."

"You are in the right place," responded Dorothy and flashed her beautiful smile. "We have nine 2-months old Gaboon adders, available for sale. They have been bred in captivity and are easy to feed and look after."

"What is the size of an adult Gaboon adder?"

"Adult snakes indigenous in SA are 1.2-1.4 meters long. But Gaboon adders from East Africa grow to 1.8 meters long. The ones on sale are from South Africa."

"And how long are their fangs?"

"The fangs for the 1.2 to 1.4 meter adders are 20 to 25 mm long. The fang record holder is the 1.8 m puff adder from East Africa, with fangs of 50 mm."

"What is the distance between the fangs?"

"It depends on the size: for small snakes, it is less than 8mm; for medium and large snakes, it is 8-13mm and more than 13 mm respectively."

"Are there pet snake owners in the US who are your clients?"

"We keep records of all our customers for regulatory reasons," said Dorothy as she sat down behind her computer. She punched a few keys and asked: "Do you recognize any of these names from Austin, Texas?"

She turned the monitor towards Paul.

There were nine names on it, with Jonathan MacDonald, listed fifth. Paul shook his head. "No, I don't know any of them." He did not want Dorothy to know that he knew Jonathan.

"Do you offer any courses on milking snakes?"

"Yes, we offer training on handling snakes, milking snakes and giving first aid for snake bites. Our chief trainer, Mr. Edmund J Benavides, has been handling snakes for over 45 years."

"Is it possible to meet Mr. Edmund Benavides?"

"He is on our snake farm right now. We keep over 600 snakes of different species for milking. I can take you there right now."

The snake farm was next door. It had a large compound and shed with cages holding various snakes. Dorothy introduced Paul as her friend from Austin, Texas, USA.

"I also have a friend from Austin called Johan Macdonald," said Mr. Benavides. "He was here for two weeks to learn how to milk snakes. He is setting up a rattlesnake farm in Austin."

Paul listened not believing his ears. He remained expressionless, not showing any emotion. "I don't know if that is the Johan I know. Do you have a picture of him?"

"Yes, come and see."

Mr. Benavides led them to a large hall with a large notice board with photos of all students who have attended courses at Serp Ent, Inc.

"Johan was here in March 2015," said Edmund. "I think it was the 5th class. Yes, here he is. He was a brilliant student."

It was indeed Johan MacDonald, holding a puff adder by the head while the rest of the class caught the middle and tail part of the viper. "No I don't know him," Paul lied. "Let me take a picture, maybe my wife may know him. He will be useful when we get our pet serpent."

Edmund showed Paul around the farm, but Paul was no longer interested. Paul's mind was on Johan. Did he milk venom and injected it into his brother? Or did he cause the snake to bite his brother when drunk or sedated? He had to find the answers.

On the farm, there were black mambas, puff adders, cobras, green snakes and many other types of venomous snakes. Each cage was labeled, with details including the kind of snake, the age, and sort of venom.

Paul Mackenzie thanked Dorothy and Edmund for their courtesy; and indicated that he would buy an exotic snake after he sorts out the required licenses.

Paul sent Jonathan's photo to his Gmail address for safety, just in case his phone got lost. He changed his departure date to Wednesday evening and spent the rest of the day looking at interesting places in South Africa.

Why would Johan want to kill his brother? That is the key to solving the puzzle. Was it rivalry over inheritance rights, money or a woman? The latter could explain the woman's shoe found at Jonathan's' on the day of his death.

Did Jonathan have business dealings with another woman or was another man involved? But why did Johan come to South Africa to learn how to milk snakes? It was confusing. Paul could not get his head to figure out what had happened.

Back in the US, Johan asked Thelma to sleep at his place on Wednesday night. Johan told Thelma that he wanted to talk. Thelma and Jonathan had worked hard to conceal their love for each other from Johan. Even if he suspected an affair between them, he did not show it.

Thelma suspected that Johan was spying on her using her phone.

She wouldn't trust him any farther than she could throw him. But how could Thelma confirm her suspicion? She did not love Johan, she loved Jonathan, but Jonathan was no more.

Could it be that Johan killed Jonathan because of jealousy? Why was Johan so bitter with her for giving the address of Jonathan's snake supplier to the Vet? The thought frightened her. But she was determined to risk her life and virginity to find out the truth.

"I will come," Thelma replied. "What time should I be there?"

"Eight o'clock in the evening," he replied.

Thelma arrived at Johan's at 8:13 pm. She knew what Johan wanted. It would cost her virginity, but Thelma wished to stop Johan from spying on her. She was determined to use trickery to protect herself.

As soon as she arrived, Johan's hands were all over her. When she saw that Johan was prepared to go all the way she unveiled the secret weapon women have used on men over the centuries.

She used the old trick on Johan: "I have always loved you, Johan. Jonathan tried hard, but he was just a flirt."

Johan looked at her in disbelief. "Really?" was his reply and continued edging her towards the sofa.

"It is not possible today because I am in my period," she said softly. "I will come back to you a few days from now."

Johan was surprised at her change of attitude. She had always resisted him. Was it because Jonathan was dead and she had no alternative? He had his doubts.

He decided not to force himself on her. It was embarrassing for Johan to undress a woman in her situation. He led her to the dining table and powered wine in two glasses.

"Wine disturbs my emotions during my monthly period," she said. "I will take tea instead."

She caught Johan unawares. He had prepared a glass special for her, with her name on it. He went to the kitchen to make her favorite cup of tea.

She stood up and followed him into the kitchen. She briefly stood between the table and Johan as if picking up her phone from the table and quickly dipped her middle finger into both glasses starting with his.

When the tea was ready, Thelma picked up a cup from the

cabinet, all the while talking excitedly with Johan. She powered herself tea and motioned Johan to follow her to the dining table.

When they went back to the table, Johan picked up her glass and showed Thelma her name engraved on the side. Thelma gave him a warm smile and thanked him for his thoughtfulness.

But it was a trick. Johan did not trust Thelma. He had smeared a sedative inside her glass to make her fall asleep. "Just taste the wine, it is a vintage red wine imported from the UK," he said. "Show how much you love me."

Thelma laughed loudly and shook her head. "I will double over in pain and spoil your evening."

Johan picked up his glass and swallowed half of it. The sedative started working within 20 minutes. He said that he felt sleepy, and attributed it to the week's grueling schedule.

Thelma proposed that they go to bed.

Thelma switched off her phone. She suspected that is a spying device. She bought the phone from a supplier Johan recommended. Johan picked the phone up from the supplier but stayed with it for over 24 hours before he gave it to Thelma.

He covered the wall clock with a hankie and switched off the TV. In the latest 2-day security training she had attended, she learned that people could employ clocks and TVs as spying devices. She scanned the ceiling and walls for hidden cameras, but there were none.

Thelma knew that the sedative would keep Johan asleep for about five hours, after that he could wake up at any moment.

She checked her watch. It was 10:15 pm.

After ascertaining that he was asleep, she opened Johan's phone by sliding his right-hand middle fingerprint over the screen.

She checked for files in the download folders, one by one. There was a list of dated media-files starting with TLM. They contained the recordings of all conversations Thelma had with people for the last eight months.

Johan had edited the list and deleted all other conversations except those she had with Jonathan, including the one in the hotel a few days before he died.

She listened to the latest one, which detailed her last conversations with Jonathan at Crystal River Inn, a Hotel located in San Marcos City.

She was astounded at what she heard. The tape started in the middle of the conversation.

"I love you, Thelma," Jonathan said. "This is my first time to fall in love."

"I love you, Jonathan," said Thelma her voice breaking a little.

Thelma was taken aback when she had her voice. It was sort of deep like the cooing of a dove.

"Will you marry me?" asked Jonathan. "I promise you all."

Some pause.

"Yes," said Thelma. "What about your brother Johan? He will kill you."

"Let me hold you closer," said Jonathan. "I will take care of him. Have you promised to marry him?"

"No," said Thelma.

Then silence.

"Have you slept with him," asked Jonathan.

"Of course not," said Thelma.

"If you choose to marry me, it will hurt him, but it is your choice," said Jonathan. "It happens all the time between brothers. He will have to accept the reality."

"Please do not do that, I am not your wife yet."

"I love you so much, I cannot imagine hurting you," said Jonathan. "Let us get out of here before I do something stupid."

The audio ended.

With shaking hands, Thelma started saving the files to her Google Drive account. Thelma confirmed that Johan had been spying on her all along using her phone.

He had listened to all their plans with Jonathan and watched as their love strengthened. I will take care of him. Was that statement the trigger that ended Jonathan's life? But he had been bitten by a snake, she thought.

She felt a cold sweat run down her spine. Was there other evidence that had prompted Jonathan's father to hire a private investigator to look into his death?

She looked at her watch. It was 2.05 am.

She had less than an hour to finish what he was doing. Thelma decided to leave all the audios as she found them. She knew Johan had backed them up somewhere else. He was too smart to have only the copy on his phone.

She cleared the download history, switched on the TV and

uncovered the wall clock. She went to bed, but could not sleep. She feared that Johan could rape her.

When Johan woke up an hour later, she also woke up and went to the bathroom. After that, she excused herself and left before dawn.

It is Monday morning, five days since Thelma slept at Johan's house. Thelma had spent the weekend pondering how Johan was able to spy on her for so long without her knowledge.

She felt cheated and betrayed but blamed herself for not dumping her phone sooner. If only I got rid of the telephone Jonathan would not have died, she thought.

She was angry. Why is the world so unfair? Why is life so cruel? Why are people so selfish?

She banged her fist on the table and promised to make Johan pay for what he had he had done to her. As she pondered the options open for her to revenge, the telephone rang.

Johan called Thelma into his office and requested her to go back to his house Thursday night.

"I will not come," she told him in a flat voice. "I am busy tonight."

"But you promised you would come," Johan retorted.

"Is it by force?" shouted Thelma. "Am I your wife?"

Johan removed his spectacles and said in a low voice: "Now listen carefully. If you are not coming to my place tonight, I will hand over the shoe you left at Jonathan's the day he died to the private investigator. You know what will happen."

"That will be blackmail," Thelma said, tears streaming down her face.

"You know what it means. You will have to explain why you were there early in the morning."

Thelma could hear the voice of her mother: "Fornication is a sin against God. If you sleep with a man before marriage, it is possibly the worst thing you can do to yourself. You become like a towel because your boyfriend ceases to see the need to obtain you legally."

"No," she shouted. "Go ahead and hand over the shoe."

Thelma was restless. Johan may have murdered Jonathan, using snake poison. She had to access Jonathan's phone and see if there was a recording of what happened on a fateful night Johan had dinner with Jonathan.

Thelma called MacDonald, Johan's Dad and asked if she could have Jonathan's phone. "I gave it to the private investigator," he said.

"There is a prospective customer I want to verify. I think I can get the address from the phone."

"Paul failed to access the phone," said MacDonald. "He has tried 12 different passwords, three more times and the phone will erase the data. He is trying to contact the phone manufacturers as a last resort."

Thelma's heart sunk. Maybe the private investigator has already given away the phone. Jonathan's phone was her only rescue. It was the only thing that could save her from jail.

She decided to take a gamble. She called Mr. Paul Mackenzie and set up a meeting at his office at 2.00pm. To her surprise, Mackenzie agreed to the meeting.

Mr. Mackenzie was middle-aged with a severe look on his face, a no-nonsense man. He reminded Thelma of Arnold Alois Schwarzenegger; an actor turned politician.

"So what is on your mind, Thelma?"

"I want to borrow Jonathan's phone to access an address for an important customer."

"Do you know the password?"

"I know the password unless Jonathan changed it before he died."

"How do you know his password?"

"I am the Administrator at MacTec10 and Jonathan was my friend."

A tear run down her cheek. She was angry, desperate and helpless. Johan had been spying on her all along and may have killed Jonathan. But she had to save herself from prison before going on the offensive.

Jonathan was dead. "We cannot help the dead," her mother used to tell her, quoting Ecclesiastes 9:5, 10. "Neither can the dead help us. They know nothing at all." She could remember the verse in the Bible because her mom quoted it many times.

Paul Mackenzie opened a cabinet and got out what looked like a phone. He unlocked the cardboard by pressed some numbers on the device. He got out a batch of keys and opened a safe across the room after turning the dial several times back and forth.

He pressed a button on his desk, and the front door to his office shut itself. "I give you only one chance," he said. "I have tried 12 times and failed. Three more times and the phone will erase all data."

Thelma punched a password, and the phone opened on her first attempt. Paul observed Thelma's hands to decipher the password. He counted the number of letters and digits: it was a combination of 11 numbers and letters. But Thelma was so fast that he could not make out the password.

"It has opened," said Thelma. "Let me get out the information I want, and I leave the phone open."

Paul Mackenzie watched in disbelief. Thelma got out her notebook. She opened a password protected folder marked "Sec Pan." She noted that the last recorded security video was on Sunday, the day before Jonathan died. She closed the folder and wrote down a fake telephone number.

She handed back the phone to Paul Mackenzie. "I have got the information I want."

"What is the password?"

"The phone is open."

"I need the password."

"I will give it to you, but I need to consult first."

Paul Mackenzie called MacDonald, but he could not reach him by phone. He had to search the phone before it was locked again.

Paul later decided against telling MacDonald about the password for the phone.

Johan called Paul Mackenzie later in the day: "I have some important information for you. Are you at the office?"

They agreed to meet in 30 minutes.

"I found the woman's shoe," said Johan. "It belongs to Thelma."

"How do you know it is Thelma's?"

"It has special mark underneath, see."

Johan showed Paul the mark. It was a label with three green letters "tlm" engraved on a red heart. It had something to do with love.

"Why would Thelma go to Jonathan's early in the morning?" asked Paul.

"Thelma had shady deals with Jonathan. They had a close relationship that I could not understand. She must know something about my brother's death."

Paul did not tell Johan that Thelma had opened Jonathan's phone.

Thelma's last phone calls to Jonathan were on Saturday at midnight and Monday morning respectively. Jonathan did not answer Thelma's phone calls.

Why would she call Jonathan at midnight? Were they in love? "Are you in love with Thelma?" asked Paul, observing Johan's reaction.

"Of course not," Johan replied and looked away. He appeared to be in deep thought. "Thelma is a weird character. She is kind of religious. I don't understand her."

"What do you mean?"

"I think she is the only virgin left in Texas."

Paul Mackenzie called Thelma and requested her to come to his office the next day.

"Why did you go to Jonathan's on the day he passed away?" asked Paul Mackenzie.

"Did Johan give you the shoe?"

Thelma started weeping. She got out a white handkerchief and wiped the tears from her face. Thelma looked beautiful in the green dress and high heels. She sat there and cried, saying nothing.

Paul Mackenzie let her weep. She would stop and start again. Her teeth were as white as cotton wool and her legs long and slender. Her waist was like that of a model. She had medium sized breasts, and long fingers with nails painted a golden color.

"Do you still have Jonathan's phone?" she asked, her dreamy eyes full of tears.

"Yes," replied Paul.

"Set up a meeting this afternoon here in your office. Make sure MacDonald and Johan are present. Invite them individually and don't tell any of them that I will be here," she said. She looked sad but beautiful. She added: "Do you have phone cables that can connect the phone to a flat screen?"

"Yes."

"Get the flat screen and cables ready. Be ready for a big show, a shocker."

When John MacDonald arrived at Paul Mackenzie's office, he was surprised to see his son Johan. "It looks as if there is going to be a big meeting," he said jokingly.

"Let us wait for one other person, and we start," said Paul Mackenzie.

Thelma arrived moments later.

They moved into Paul Mackenzie's lecture theatre on the same floor. It had a 42" flat screen, chairs and a whiteboard.

"I want to show you a video," Thelma began, "to clear my name. I was the first at the scene on the day Jonathan died, but I have nothing to do with his death. I loved him so much."

No one said a word; they didn't know what to expect.

"I have already connected the phone," said Mackenzie, "just start the video."

Thelma found the video and clicked on the 'play' icon. There was deafening silence for about thirty seconds and then heavy footsteps as if someone carrying a heavy load was going upstairs.

Johan appeared, carrying Jonathan on his shoulder. He placed Jonathan on the couch and got out the snake handling equipment from the drawer. He was wearing rubber gloves.

"Call Thelma for me," said Jonathan, in a weak but clear voice. Jonathan tried to get off the couch, but he could not move. He lay down again and slept. Jonathan appeared sedated.

Johan got a V-shaped jar out of the drawer. Tied tightly over the glass container was a piece of white cloth. Johan carefully placed it in its holder on the table and went back to the drawer. He got out snake tongs, overalls, a collapsible hook, eye protection and a bag, and neatly laid them on the table beside the jar holder.

Johan put on the overalls, eye protection, picked up a snake catcher and opened the snake cage. He threw in a small rat, and a medium-size puff adder came out of its hiding. It was Jonathan's pet snake. He grabbed the snake a third way from the head using the tongs and lifted it out of the cage.

He placed the fat, relatively short snake on the floor. They could hear the noise as it hissed and wriggled. He kept a safe distance away. He used the hook to hold down the snake by its neck and held the latch down using his foot.

In a swift move, Johan grabbed the snake just behind the head and let go of the snake tong. The snake opened its mouth baring its deadly fangs. Johan made the snake bite through the cloth, releasing venom into the jar. He milked the snake three times before taking the snake back to the cage.

He threw it back into the cage and closed it. He took a syringe, fixed on a 40 mm needle (cream in color) and sucked the deadly venom into a 5ml syringe.

Johan stood and looked around, white-faced, like a ghost. His face was expressionless as death. He mercilessly pushed the needle into the lower part of Jonathan's leg and injected the venom into Jonathan's flesh. Jonathan moved slightly but did not wake up.

Johan pulled out the needle and again filled it with venom and injected Jonathan a second time, close to the first puncture hole to mimic a snake bite.

He put back the equipment into the drawer, removed the needle from the syringe and carefully inserted it back into its sheath. He put the jar, syringe, and needle in a plastic bag opened the snake cage door and walked out of the room, holding the plastic bag.

The recording continued, but there was dead silence. Jonathan stayed motionless on the coach. His cat slept in the corner.

Paul Mackenzie stood up, switched off the video and returned to his seat.

As the recording progressed, people reacted in disbelief, glued to the big screen as if their life depended on it. There were gasps...silence..."Oh no!" Some noises were unintelligible. At one time someone cried: "You monster" but no one moved from his seat.

When Johan mercilessly injected his brother with snake venom, MacDonald put his hands on his head, not believing what he was he was seeing. "My God," he shouted. Johan had turned into a beast. MacDonald started weeping silently.

At one time everyone in the room gasped as Johan inserted the needle into Jonathan's flesh and carefully injected the deadly venom. Johan started for the door, but it was locked. "Sit down and do not move," yelled MacDonald. Johan who was trembling like tea leaves in a sieve obeyed his father's voice and sat down.

Mackenzie watched calmly, taking in every detail. His face was twisted in pain, his hands firmly grasping his chair. What he was seeing was worse than a horror movie. At the back of your mind, you know that horror movies are fiction, but this was real.

Thelma screamed now and again throughout the recording. She saw Johan dismantling her love affair bit by bit. He had no compassion; he was merciless. At one time she started blaming herself. She was the cause of all this. She fainted in her chair when Johan pushed snake venom into Jonathan's body, but no one noticed.

Everyone sat in silence.

MacDonald was sobbing loudly.

Ten minutes passed.

"Johan, why did you do it," asked Paul Mackenzie.

"Jonathan took away the only girl I loved," Johan whispered. "I love Thelma with all my heart. When Jonathan proposed to Thelma, I went mad. Anger overpowered me. I killed my brother to get back Thelma. I thought no one would know."

Thelma gained consciousness. She got her shoe and hit Johan on the head. "You have destroyed my life, you fool," she shouted. "I hate you. You installed spying software on my phone. You eavesdropped on all our conversations with Jonathan. You deserve to die."

Paul Mackenzie held Thelma by the hand and pulled her away from Johan.

"What if I had slept with him?" she asked. "I think you would have killed yourself. But I didn't. You killed an innocent man; you are a coward." She cried the more, tears freely rolling down her cheeks.

"What have you done me, Johan?" Macdonald asked his son. "You have destroyed my business and my family." He covered his face and wept loudly.

"Forgive me, Dad," Johan begged, tears rolling down his cheeks. He knelt before his father. "It was anger. I regret it. Please have mercy on me don't hand me over to Police."

MacDonald stopped crying and looked at Johan intently.

"Look I bore only two sons," MacDonald began, his voice breaking now and then. "They fought for Thelma and Johan killed Jonathan. And now I have to hand over my remaining son, the only one, to the Police to be jailed for life. The two of them have been the brain behind MacTec10. Life can be cruel."

He wept some more. Paul Mackenzie moved next to MacDonald and let him cry on his shoulder. It was difficult to imagine how MacDonald felt as he went through the ordeal.

"No, I will not hand over my son. My business has to continue."

"But he a murderer," said Thelma. "If you don't know, you may be the next on his hit list. Johan has tasted human blood; he can do it again. You are putting all our lives in danger."

"You must hand over Johan to face justice," said Paul Mackenzie. "If the law catches up with you, you can go to jail for covering up a murderer."

Mackenzie pulled out a photo from an envelope and handed it to MacDonald: "I got this from South Africa. Can you recognize who is learning to handle and milk snakes?"

"This is Johan," said MacDonald in a low voice. "You went to South Africa?"

"Yes, I did,"

Dead Silence. Johan did not move or utter a word.

MacDonald repeated, his voice full of surprise and anger: "Johan, you went to South Africa to prepare for your brother's death?"

Johan did not answer. He just looked straight ahead as if dead.

"It was premeditated murder," MacDonald said in a low voice.

MacDonald stood up and started pacing the room.

Finally, he drew in a deep breath and said: "No, I will not hand over Johan."

Paul Mackenzie was dismayed. "Bless your heart," he said.

Johan managed a fake smile. It was one of those smiles you switch on and off.

"Now I know that money and blood taste sweeter than justice," Thelma said scornfully. "For today, you have chosen to shield Johan from facing justice."

It is time I start preparing my revenge, thought Thelma. "'Vengeance is mine,' says Jehovah. 'I will repay.'" Her mother's voice rung clear in her mind. You should forgive and never keep a grudge, said her mother.

"Mr. Mackenzie, please keep Jonathan's phone safe," said Thelma calmly. "We shall need it to save our necks."

Thelma was determined to avenge Jonathan's death.

ABOUT THE AUTHOR

Robertello Matousek worked as an industrial engineer for many years before switching careers to finance, accounting and banking. He is currently a freelance consultant in finance, accounting, leasing, and engineering. He also enjoys speaking at public events on a wide range of topics including economics and science-related subjects.
Beside number crunching, he has been engaged in voluntary work, helping local communities in several African countries. He is keenly interested in nature and environmental conservation. He enjoys reading novels and spends a substantial amount of his money on books. He is the author of the novel, "Trek of Death, Trek of Hope."

www.ingramcontent.com/pod-product-compliance
Lightning Source LLC
Chambersburg PA
CBHW071352130626
46556CB00005B/2144